FIREMAN SAM
AND THE FOUNTAIN

story by Diane Wilmer
illustrations by the County Studio

HEINEMANN · LONDON

Pontypandy Park had been open for a hundred years.

"It's the centenary next week," said Station Officer Steele. "We must do something really special to celebrate the event."

"Bella's organised a party," said Fireman Sam.

"Hmm," said Station Officer Steele. "We need something extra special, that no one else will have thought of."

"I've got it!" said Fireman Sam. "We can mend the fountain in the park. You know, the one in the middle, just near the bandstand. It's not worked for years. We could get it going and paint it up, it'd look a real treat."

"Jolly good," said Station Officer Steele. "Let's get cracking, we've not a minute to waste."

The day of the centenary came and it was boiling hot.

"PHEW!" gasped Fireman Elvis Cridlington as he buttoned up his heavy uniform. "I could do with a swim."

"Not now, Cridlington," said Station Officer Steele. "Let's just concentrate on the fountain for the moment."

"Well, I hope it works," said Fireman Sam as he oiled up the old pump.

"Of course it'll work, it just needs a bit of organisation!" said Station Officer Steele. "Cridlington will be here, in the control shed. You'll be standing at the back of the crowd and after I've given my speech and cut the ribbon tied around the fountain, you'll wave to Cridlington and he'll turn on the water. Easy as blinking!"

"It's not quite that simple, Sir," said Fireman Sam.

"Some of these workings are pretty old, they might jam after all these years."

"Nonsense!" laughed Station Officer Steele. "Everything will be fine!"

The band played and people began to wander up the hill to the park.

"Come on, James!" called Sarah. "Or we'll be late for the opening ceremony."

"Quick!" yelled Norman, "Station Officer Steele is just about to start his speech."

"Hum . . . hum . . . hum . . . hum!" said Station Officer Steele. "Thank you all for coming to the opening of the Park Fountain. My men and I have worked very hard to restore it and we hope that you will be as proud of it as we are!" He cut the red ribbon and smiled.

"I now declare this fountain well and truly open!"

"Hurray! Hurray!" cheered the children.

"Well done, boys!" cried Trevor Evans.

"There's beautiful," smiled Dilys.

Fireman Sam gave the thumbs up sign to Elvis, who turned the wheel – but nothing happened.

"Er . . . I now declare this fountain, er, well and truly . . . OPEN!" yelled Station Officer Steele. Still nothing happened. "What's going on?" he hissed.

Fireman Sam shrugged his shoulders. "I don't know but I'll try and find out," he said.

He found Elvis struggling with the big wheel.

"What's up?" he asked.

"The bloomin' thing's jammed," said Elvis. "I can't move it."

"Give it a bash with your hammer," said Fireman Sam. "That should shift it alright."

"OK," said Elvis and whacked the wheel with his hammer. C–L–A–N–G!

Meanwhile Station Officer Steele was peering into the centre of the fountain.

"Just hold on," he was saying. "I'll soon have this sorted out."

Whoooosh! The water came shooting up and hit him smack in the face.

"Well, that's one way of cooling off!" said Trevor Evans.

"Can we all join in?" asked Norman.

"Certainly not!" dripped Station Officer Steele. "The fountain's only for fish."

Norman peered into the big, stone bowl. "I can't see any fish," he said.

"They're here," said James and he tipped some goldfish out of a plastic bag into the water.

"Where did they come from?" asked Norman.

"From the pond," said Sarah. "Look I've got some too." She tipped her bag into the water and with a flick of their tails the fish went darting off.

"Quack! Quack!" went some ducks and landed with a splash in the fountain.

Norman watched the ducks. "I'd like a paddle too," he thought and hid behind the bushes.

The band began to play and everyone slowly wandered over to the bandstand to listen to the music.

"Are you coming down to my party later?" Bella asked the firemen.

"We'll be down when we've finished this shift," said Fireman Sam.

"Where's Norman?" asked Sarah.

"He's probably run on ahead to sample the ice-cream!" laughed Trevor.

As soon as they'd all gone Norman slipped out from his hiding place and jumped into the fountain.

"Whoopee!" he cried as he danced in and out of the splashing water. "Cool at last...wheeee!"

Suddenly he heard a voice.

"Hello there Norman! I thought you'd gone back to Bella's?"

"*Ooh*, Elvis!" gulped Norman. "What are you doing here?"

"I had to stay behind and fix this bloomin' fountain," said Elvis. "But look what I found..." He held up an old football. "Here – catch!" The ball came whizzing towards Norman who caught it and sent it flying back to Elvis. Then Elvis kicked it really high. It landed, PLOP, right on top of the fountain.

"WOW! What a shot!" giggled Norman.

"Oh dear, it's stuck up there," said Elvis.

"Don't worry, I'll get it," said Norman.

But the ball was slowly slipping down inside the fountain-head.

"Quick, grab it!" yelled Elvis.

GLUG! went the ball and disappeared down the pipe.

"Well, that's the end of that," said Elvis. "Better not tell anybody, Norman or we'll both be in trouble."

"OK, mum's the word," said Norman, pressing his finger to his lips.

"Mum's the word," said Elvis with a wink.

When Elvis arrived back at the Fire Station, he had to clean all the windows.

"Well, at least it's a cool job," he thought. "Better be quick though, or I'll miss all the fun down in Pontypandy."

Station Officer Steele was thinking the same thing. "I'll finish my filing then go down to Bella's," he thought, but his room was very hot. "PHEW!" he gasped and threw open the window. He stood there, trying to cool down, when along came Elvis, singing at the top of his voice.

Without looking up, Elvis picked up his bucket of water and whizzed it straight at the window – *whooosh!* The water went flying and hit Station Officer Steele right in the face.

"AAAGHH!" he roared.

Elvis dropped his bucket and started to tremble.

"Oh my giddy aunt!" he gulped. "I... er... I thought the window was shut!"

"Well it wasn't!" cried Station Officer Steele. "This is the second time you've drenched me today."

"It was an accident," said Elvis. "I promise it won't ever happen again."

"Hummmph! Well just make sure it doesn't," said Station Officer Steele. "Otherwise you'll be in big trouble, Fireman Cridlington. Now hurry up and get those windows finished, at the double!"

Down at Bella's cafe the party was in full swing.

"Delicious!" said Trevor, tucking into more sandwiches.

"Now, now, Trevor, don't eat everything," scolded Dilys. "The firemen haven't arrived yet."

"Come on," said Sarah to James. "Let's go up to the park and have a look at our fish."

It was quiet in the park and very, very hot.

"That's funny," said James as they walked along the path. "I can't hear the fountain. It was quite loud when we left."

Sarah stood still and listened. "I can't hear anything either," she said.

They stared at each other, thinking exactly the same thing. "The FISH!" they cried and ran to the fountain.

They found the fish flopping about in a tiny bit of water, all that was left in the bottom of the big, stone bowl.

"Quick," said James. "We must scoop them out and put them in the pond."

"Oh dear," said Sarah. "Do you think they'll be all right?"

The fish were still for a while then they slowly began to move around the pond.

"They're fine," said James. "But I think we'd better tell Uncle Sam about the fountain."

"Poor Uncle Sam, he'll be really fed up," said Sarah. "He's been working all day."

Fireman Sam *was* fed up. "Oh daro!" he said. "I was just about to leave for Bella's party."

"I'd better come with you," said Station Officer Steele. "Elvis is still busy cleaning the windows."

They climbed into Jupiter and Fireman Sam drove them down the hill to the park.

"Hey! Where are you going?" yelled Elvis.

"To the park," said Station Officer Steele. "The fountain's blocked up again."

"Again?" said Elvis, then he remembered. "Oh no, the ball!" he cried. "HEY! Wait for me!"

But it was too late. Fireman Sam had turned the corner and was thundering down the hill to Pontypandy.

"HELP!" spluttered Elvis. "If Station Officer Steele finds that ball, there'll be big trouble!"

Fireman Sam and Station Officer Steele were very puzzled.

"I don't know what the problem is," said Fireman Sam. "I've checked everything. The blockage must be up top."

Station Officer Steele peered into the fountain-head. "I can't see a thing down there," he said.

"I'll tell you what, Sir," said Fireman Sam. "I'll switch the pump onto maximum and see if that helps."

They all waited while Fireman Sam turned up the pump, but nothing happened.

"What's going on?" called Station Officer Steele.

"I don't know," answered Fireman Sam. "I'll pump up more water, maybe the increased water pressure will push the blockage through."

Again they waited but still nothing happened.

"It's well and truly blocked this time," said James.

"It's very strange," said Fireman Sam. "The water's going through all right, I can hear it loud and clear, but it's not coming out the other end."

Suddenly a loud rumble came from the control shed.

"Uh-oh!" cried Fireman Sam. "Sounds like we've got problems." He grabbed the wheel to turn the water off, but as he turned it the wheel broke off in his hands.

At that moment Elvis came racing up the hill towards them. "Stop!" he gasped. "S T O P!"

But nobody was listening to him. The rumble changed to a roar as the water thundered through the pipes.

"Oh, Uncle Sam!" cried Sarah. "What's happening?"

"The pressure's building up," said Fireman Sam. "It's got to come up somewhere."

"Yes, but WHERE is the question," said Station Officer Steele.

Suddenly a manhole cover just beneath the bandstand shot up into the air. WHOOOOSH! The water came bubbling up in a great fountain.

"Stand clear! Stand clear!" yelled Fireman Sam.

There was no stopping the water. It rushed out of the pipes down the path, straight towards Pontypandy.

Elvis ran over to the fountain. "It's OK," he said. "I can fix it."
He climbed onto the fountain and reached down inside it.

"Got it!" he cried, pulling out the ball with a loud POP!

"This is no time for silly games, Cridlington," said Station
Officer Steele. "Just what do you think you're up to?"

"I'll explain later," said Elvis and quickly jumped down.
"Watch out, here it comes!"

The water came shooting up out of the fountain and
splashed into the stone bowl.

"Thank goodness for that," said Fireman Sam. "Now give me a hand with the manhole cover."

They all helped Fireman Sam lift the heavy lid and put it back over the manhole.

"Is it safe Uncle Sam?" asked Sarah.

"It's safe now," said Fireman Sam. "The water from the fountain has taken the pressure off the pipes. We'll have everything back to normal in no time."

"But what about the wheel?" asked James. "Won't you have to mend it?"

"Yes, I'll have to get some welding equipment from the fire station," said Fireman Sam. "I'll come and mend it later."

"Come on," said Station Officer Steele. "Let's go down to Pontypandy and see if any damage has been done."

In the village they found the main street awash.

"*WHHEEE!* This is great!" cried Norman as he splashed about. "Just like the seaside."

"Norman, get out of the way," said Station Officer Steele. "We've got to pump this lot up."

Elvis got the hoses out. He put one into the water and the other into the river.

"Rightio," he called. "Switch on the pump."

Fireman Sam operated the controls, as one of the hoses
sucked in the water and the other pumped it out into the
river. In no time the street was clear.

"Well done!" called Dilys.

"Jolly good!" boomed Trevor Evans.

"Bravo!" cried Bella.

"Now Elvis, perhaps you'd like to tell me about the football
in the fountain?" said Station Officer Steele.

Elvis looked uncomfortable. "Well," he said. "Norman and I were having a game of football earlier on this afternoon and the ball sort of . . . er . . ."

"Got stuck on top of the fountain," continued Norman.

"Got stuck!" snapped Station Officer Steele. "You were on duty, Cridlington. What were you doing playing football?"

"Oh! it wasn't him," interrupted Norman. "It was me that kicked the ball. He just kicked it back."

"And when he kicked it back it went straight inside the fountain?" asked Fireman Sam. "You were never much good at football, were you, Elvis?"

Norman giggled, but Station Officer Steele looked annoyed.

"Come on, let's not argue today," smiled Bella and led the way into her cafe.

"Look, all your favourite things," she said.

"Mmmm . . . this is lovely," said Fireman Sam.

"Phew! I thought I was in trouble then," whispered Elvis.

Norman winked and pressed his finger to his lips. "Mum's the word," he said.

"Have you tried my spicy pizza?" Bella asked Station Officer Steele.

"No, but I'd certainly like to," he replied.

"Watch out for it," warned Trevor Evans. "It's a bit on the hot side."

"Oh, that won't worry me," said Station Officer Steele and he bit into the pizza. "AAAAGHHH!" he cried. "Water! Water!"

Elvis grabbed a glass of water and handed it to Station Officer Steele.

"Water, Sir," he said. "There's plenty of that in Pontypandy!"

FIREMAN SAM SAYS:

Football is a good game but only
play in wide open spaces where you
won't break anything if you miss
the ball.

William Heinemann Ltd, Michelin House,
81 Fulham Road, London SW3 6RB

LONDON   MELBOURNE   AUCKLAND

First published 1990 by William Heinemann Ltd
Text copyright © 1990 William Heinemann Ltd
Illustrations copyright © 1990 William Heinemann Ltd
Fireman Sam copyright © 1985 Prism Art & Design Ltd
All rights reserved
Based on the animation series produced by Bumper
Films for S4C/Channel 4 Wales and Prism Art & Design Ltd
Original idea by Dave Gingell and Dave Jones, assisted
by Mike Young   Characters created by Rob Lee
ISBN (HB) 434 97333 5   (PB) 434 97334 3
Printed in Great Britain by Cambus Litho, East Kilbride